THE ENORMOUS CARROT

THE CARROT FEAST

THE ENORMO

US CARROT

Vladimir Vagin

SCHOLASTIC PRESS/NEW YORK

Library of Congress Cataloging-in-Publication Data
Vagin, Vladimir Vasil'evich, 1937-
The enormous carrot   Vladimir Vagin. — 1st ed.
p.   cm.
Summary : A group learns the value of teamwork as one animal
after another joins in the effort to pull a giant carrot out of
the ground. Based on a Russian folktale.
ISBN 0-590-45491-9
[1. Folklore—Russia.] I. Title.
PZ8.1.V35En   1998   398.2'0497'02—dc21
[E]   97-14770   CIP AC
10 9 8 7 6 5 4 3 2 1   89   90   0 01 02 03

Printed in the U.S.A.   37
First edition, April 1998
The illustrations for this book were created with
colored pencil and watercolor.
The text type was set in Elroy.
Design by Kristina Iulo

Early one spring, Daisy and Floyd planted seeds in their garden.

Each day, they watered and weeded.

Everything grew exactly as they had planned.

Then one morning . . .

Daisy and Floyd discovered an enormous carrot
growing in the middle of their garden.

"This carrot is ready to pick," said Floyd.

So Floyd tried to pull the carrot out of the ground.

But the carrot stayed put.

It wouldn't come out.

"I'll pull it out," said Daisy.

Daisy tried to pull the carrot out of the ground.

But the carrot stayed put.

It wouldn't come out.

Then Daisy and Floyd tried together
to pull the carrot out of the ground.

They tugged and they lugged.
But the carrot stayed put. It wouldn't come out.

Just then, their friend Mabel came by.

"Will you help us pull this carrot out?" asked Daisy.

"Naturally," said Mabel.

So Daisy, Floyd, and Mabel tried together
to pull the enormous carrot out of the ground.
They heaved and they ho'd.
But the carrot stayed put. It wouldn't come out.

Just then, their friend Henry came by.

"Will you help us pull this carrot out?" asked Mabel.

"Glad to," said Henry.

So Daisy, Floyd, Mabel, and Henry tried together
to pull the enormous carrot out of the ground.
They grunted and they groaned.
But the carrot stayed put. It wouldn't come out.

Just then, their friend Gloria came by.

"Will you help us pull this carrot out?" asked Henry.

"Absolutely," said Gloria.

So Daisy, Floyd, Mabel, Henry, and Gloria
tried together to pull the enormous carrot out of the ground.
They teamed and they towed.
But the carrot stayed put. It wouldn't come out.

Just then, their friend Buster came by.

"Will you help us pull this carrot out?" asked Gloria.

"Sure thing," said Buster.

So Daisy, Floyd, Mabel, Henry, Gloria, and Buster
tried together to pull the enormous carrot out of the ground.
They stretched and they swayed.
But the carrot stayed put. It wouldn't come out.

Just then, their friend Claire came by.

"Will you help us pull this carrot out?" asked Buster.

"I'd be delighted," said Claire.

So Daisy, Floyd, Mabel, Henry, Gloria, Buster, and Claire
tried together to pull the enormous carrot out of the ground.
They hollered and they hauled.
But the carrot stayed put. It wouldn't come out.

Just then, their friend Lester came by.

"May I help you pull that carrot out?" asked Lester.

"You're much too small!" said Claire.

"Let me try," said Lester.

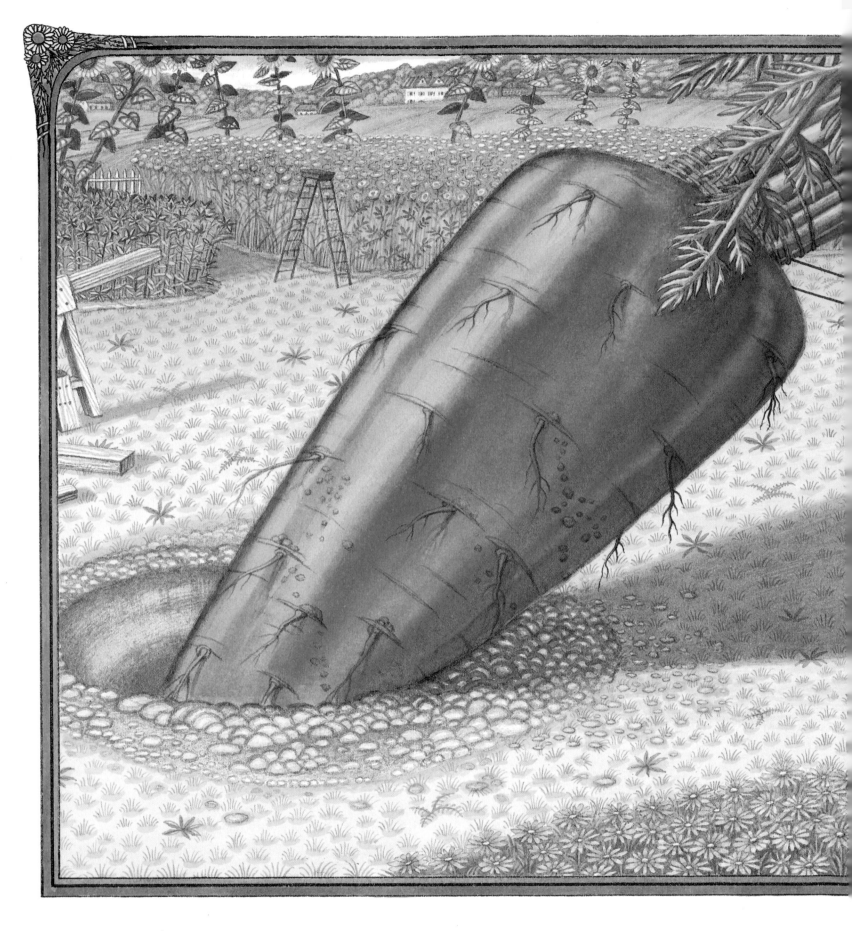

So Daisy, Floyd, Mabel, Henry, Gloria, Buster, Claire, and Lester
tried together to pull the enormous carrot out of the ground.
They tugged and they lugged,
they heaved and they ho'd,
they grunted and they groaned,

they teamed and they towed,

they stretched and they swayed,

they hollered and they hauled,

and all at once . . .

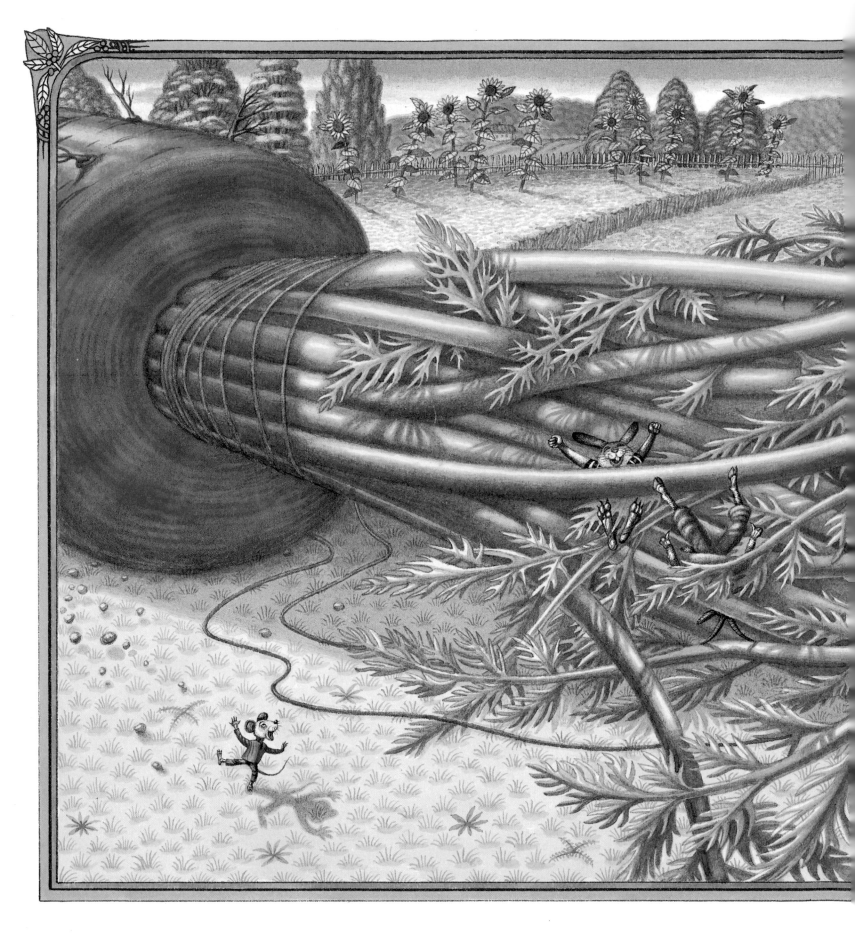

the enormous carrot...

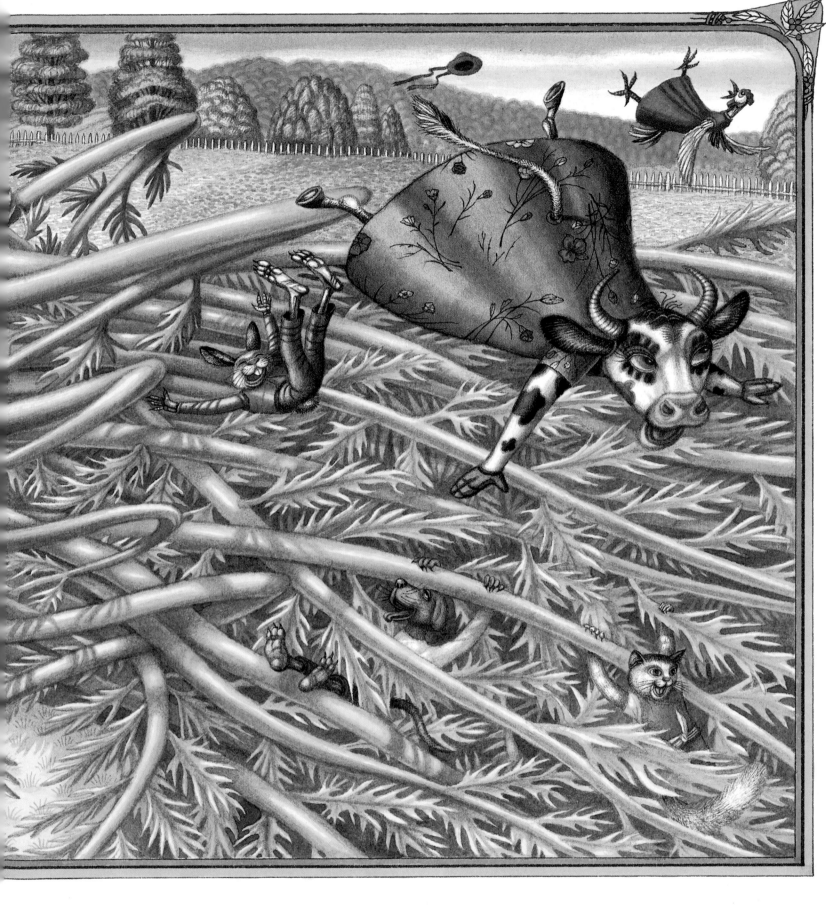

CAME OUT!

Then Daisy, Floyd, Mabel, Henry, Gloria, Buster, Claire, Lester, and all

their friends ate every bit of that enormous carrot until it was all gone.

That afternoon, Daisy said, "I can't wait to see what comes up tomorrow."
"Neither can I," said Floyd. "But first it's time for an ENORMOUS REST."